# THE

# MAN

Donovan Hurst

Cover Image: Unknown Man

Printed 2013

Copyright © 2012 Donovan Hurst Books

United States

ISBN: 0985696893
ISBN-13: 978-0-9856968-9-4

# Dedication

To my family who have given their continued
love & support

# Contents

# The Wagon

The sun rose from behind the clouds.
The air tumbled blindly, shaking the tree
tops.  The creaking of wooden wheels
grinding small sticks and leaves on the
ground echoed through the forest.  The
wagon moved forward at a steady pace.
The driver held the reigns of the horse
with one hand as he used the other hand
to push his hat down on his head to keep
it from blowing away.  The air seemed
warmer this year than last year.

The driver of the wagon had seen many

things in his long life, but still maintained a youthful appearance. His brown beard was neatly trimmed and still did not show any shades of grey. He wore a light-weight leather coat over his white linen shirt and green culottes. Remarkably his clothes looked as if they had just been washed and pressed, even though he had been driving the wagon for so many days that he could not remember.

The horse stopped suddenly. The driver did not notice the horse standing motionless. He had been on this journey for such a long time that he could not tell that that horse had stopped; he could feel her still walking, pulling him and the wagon onward. It was not until he heard a voice in the foreground that his automated state shattered and he was brought back to the here and now.

"… you must pay…" was all the driver heard before he looked up from his hands holding the reigns to his horse. A man holding a match-lock musket stood in front of him. The man looked liked he had not bathed in days and had been living in the wild all of his life. He was dressed in a long sleeve cotton shirt with animal skin pants. Behind the man with the musket were a couple of logs laid out in the middle of the path. A crude barricade, but effective none the less, especially when

3

four other men are standing by the logs. The four men looked the same as the man with the match-lock musket. Two of them were standing on the right of the logs. Each man held a long knife, with a second knife holstered in their belts. The other two men were standing on the left of the logs. Each man held a flint-lock pistol with a knife holstered in their belts.

"Did you hear me?" the man with the match-lock musket asked. The driver of the wagon sat motionless. The driver loosened his hold of the reigns and slowly placed his hands on his lap.

"I said, this is the road of Peter the

Great Huntsmen, which is me, and you must pay Peter the Great Huntsmen a tax for using his road.  If you do not have any gold then we will take the cargo in your wagon."

"Well, then we have a problem.  I have no gold and I have no cargo." the driver replied.

"That is hard to believe, since one of my associates happened to see you leaving the tavern not that long ago, and he saw much treasure in your wagon."

"He was probably drunk.  I carry no treasure and I have not stopped anywhere since I left the stable where I was hired to drive this wagon."

"Is that so? Harry look in the wagon."

Harry walked from the left, holding his pistol loosely aimed at the driver as he walked to the back of the wagon to inspect the cargo. Harry reached the back of the wagon and peered over the top. The wagon was empty. Dumbfounded, he looked again. He had the same result. The wagon was empty. Harry walked back to the front of the wagon. Once he was face to face with the driver he motioned for the driver to get down from the wagon. The driver obliged, carefully placing the two reigns on the seat as he descended from the wagon.  Loosely holding the pistol in front of the driver, Harry spoke softly.

"It's empty."  Harry said to the driver in a low tone.

"I know."

With those words the driver knocked Harry down as he grabbed the pistol from his hand and knife from the belt.  Harry fell onto his back.  The sound of leaves rustling and twigs breaking was interrupted with the explosion of powder from the pan as the flint grinded of the strike plate.  Before he could react, the bullet struck Peter in the head, killing him instantly.  The round iron ball hit its target with deadly accuracy.

Harry had regained his feet and lunged at the driver. The driver moved out of the way slicing Harry's throat with the knife. Harry fell hitting the side of the wagon as he collapsed. The man on the left of the log fired his pistol at the driver. The bullet missed, ricocheting off the top of the side board of the wagon. The two men on the right of the logs charged the driver with their knives held high. The driver parried each of their attacks. The driver grabbed one of the men's knives from their belt as he dodged their attack. As the two men prepared to attack, the driver was ready, armed with the two knives he had retrieved from his attackers. With lightening quickness the driver blocked the incoming blows from the men. In the process the driver stabbed each man in the heart. The last man had dropped his discharged pistol and made way to the match-lock musket that was still in the hands of its owner Peter. The man freed the weapon and began to raise the musket to fire at the driver. Before he could raise the musket to his shoulder to fire, a knife was thrown with great velocity through the air, piercing the hand of the attacker. The knife penetrated his hand and lodged itself into the butt of the musket. Before the man could scream in pain, a second knife pierced his throat stopping itself in the man's spine. The driver surveyed the scene as he caught his breath. Five men were dead, he was unharmed. The driver climbed back into the seat of the wagon and picked up the reigns. He snapped the reigns signaling the horse to move on. The wagon maneuvered itself passed the logs in the road and continued on the path through the forest.

The air became cooler. The wagon proceeded out of the forest and rolled on into a clearing. A faint sound of rippling water echoed in the distance. The horse instinctively walked on toward the running water. By mid day the horse and driver

were taking in the cool crisp water of the
stream. The wagon was parked with small
logs placed under the back two wheels in
order to keep the wagon from rolling
forward. The horse was unhitched and
walked casually back and forth from the
wagon to the stream. The driver piled a
group of small sticks together and found
some stones along the bank of the stream,
which he used to make a circle around the
sticks. Within a few moments a small fire
was burning in the recently made hearth
with a couple of skewed fish roasting in
the fire. As the horse grazed alongside the
stream the driver dined on the two pieces
of fish. After his meal, he walked past the

horse.

"We will spend some time here my old friend.  It has been a long day and there is still much distance to travel." he quietly said to the horse as he made his way to the stream.

"*Why do people try to take what is not theirs to have?*" he kept thinking to himself as he bent forward pulling off his leather boots as he stood next to the stream.  He tossed each boot on to the ground and walked into the cool running water.  After exiting the stream the driver had found a large tree stump to lean his back against as he drifted into another dream state.

# I ./././././

The man grabbed his suit coat tightly around him during the night as he slept and the temperature became cooler. His suit pants were wrinkled as well as his shirt, after all he was sleeping on a park bench.

The man stirred as the sound of men's footsteps came closer toward him. The men's footsteps echoed loudly through the trees as they walked on the cobblestone and concrete walkway, which would lead them directly to him.

# The Soldier

The artillery shell burst overhead, knocking the private first class to the ground. He looked down to make sure he still held his M-1 Garand rifle. He slowly raised his left arm and straightened his helmet. He could not tell where the rest of his squad was. Every man scattered after the first shell burst. Returning to his knees he began to survey the scene. Black clouds of smoke appeared overhead with each new burst of artillery. The trees shook violently.  Splinters of wood and leaves fluttering throughout the sky as many of the surrounding trees were struck by an occasional exploding shell.

"*Get up.  Get up now*!" a voice inside his head commanded.

"*Move your feet, soldier!  Move! Move! Move!*" the voice continued.

The soldier got on his feet and made a V line for the trees that were opposite of the direction the artillery shells were being fired from.  Seeming like an eternity, the soldier ran a few hundred yards into the forest.  Reaching safety for the moment, the soldier crouched down next the first available thing, which happened to be a partially intact tree stump. He was comforted by the sound of quiet. The artillery shells seemed to have ceased for the now. The smoke was clearing and the sunlight trickled through the branches of leaves.

He grabbed his map from a side pocket and began looking for the coordinates for the rally point. He did not have that much time before the enemy's artillery shells would begin another round. Quickly stashing the map back into his side pocket, the soldier began running in the direction of the rally point. It seemed like an eternity, but finally the soldier reached his destination.

"Flash." said the soldier as he slowly crept into the rally point area. He was expecting to hear one of his buddies reply with the code word "Thunder", but there was no response.

*"Where could they be?"* he thought to himself as he continued onward becoming more anxious and nervous as he made each step.

"Flash."

No response.

"Flash."

No response.

The soldier stopped, leaning his tired body on a massive tree trunk.  He looked to the heavens with eyes closed and with one last ounce of desperation he uttered one more, "Flash."

"Thunder."

Snapping his head down, the soldier saw some slight rustling of leaves and tree limbs coming from the right said of the forest.  A feeling of hope washed over him as he saw a fellow soldier from his squad. PFC Raines emerged from the bushes.  He was very stout and muscular, which lead to him earning the nickname "Hoss".  He also was always given the manual labor assignments when the squad was stationed at camp.

"I am sure glad to see you." Hoss told the soldier.

"I did not think that I would ever find anyone after the shells starting flying."

"I am glad to see you too. You are the first person I have seen in a long while. We better keep moving and find our way to the next rally point. I would think that command would have set up another headquarters by now. Plus I do not want to keep holding on to this satchel."

The soldier opened up a few buttons of his shirt, exposing a piece of a dark leather object where his chest would have been, to Hoss.

"You still have that?" Hoss exclaimed surprised.

"I thought Sarge would have given that thing to someone else, after the incident."

"Well you thought wrong. Even though I don't want it, this item was given to me. Maybe after all of this is over I'll understand why, but for now we better keep moving."

"I guess you are right. I was looking

over the map before I ran into you and the next rally point is that way." Hoss stated pointing to the west.

Both men walked through the forest, in silence with weapons at the ready. They did not known for certain if they were alone. Throughout their journey they would alternate saying the code word "Flash".

They stopped at a small clearing where a tiny creek was slowly running. The soldier knelt by the edge of the water and tried taking a drink of the water. Hoss stood at the point. Leaves began rustling off in the distance, hopeful that it was more members of their squad; Hoss called out "Flash" to the direction of the noise.

"Flash."

No response.

"Flash," Hoss spoke again and then turned to the soldier, who was just getting to his feet.

"I think we found another …"

A bullet exploded out of Hoss' windpipe causing a cloud of red to dance through the air. Another bullet struck him in the leg.

The soldier immediately opened fired as he ran toward his injured comrade. When he reached the point where Hoss was struck, Hoss fell into his arms, shock setting in with deep gasps of air trying to bring oxygen into his already failing lungs. The soldier looked into Hoss' eyes as another bullet entered his skull killing him instantly.

Before he could react to the fatal blow, he was already surrounded by five members of the enemy's forces.

"Put your weapon down," the enemy Captain ordered to the soldier in an almost perfect English accent.

There was no use in resisting, for he was surrounded. His weapon lay silently on the ground as he was violently shoved by two of the soldier's MP40 butt stocks in his back and ribs.

"Put him over there by that tree and secure his hands. You two keep watch over there. We don't want any more of his friends showing up unannounced."

"Yes sir." The other two soldiers replied and walked off in the direction the Captain ordered them to go. By the time they left, the soldier was leaning on the trunk of a large tree with his hands crudely lashed behind his own back.

"Now we will see what he has been carrying for it must be important for me to have been ordered to fetch it.  Do you know that we have been watching your every move for some time now?”

The soldier began to drift off, losing all attention in what was happening around him.

“Search him!” yelled the Captain, bringing the soldier back to the current situation.

One of the Gerry’s swung his MP40 onto his back as he moved to the soldier. He began slowly patting him down in order to find the package.  He reached his boots and turned to the Captain shaking his head as if saying there was nothing there.

"Search him again.  We know he has it."

The Gerry again searched the soldier, but achieved the same result.

"Do I have to do everything myself? Step aside you idiot," the Captain said shoving the Gerry back.  Gerry I shrugged as he regained his balance after being shoved aside by the Captain.  Gerry II moved over to Gerry I to see if he was okay because he had been on many of the Captain's shoving sprees during his time in the service.  Gerry III and IV were still keeping watch a large distance away. They had no idea of what was happening and could not sense what impending doom they were all in.

The Captain stood face to face with the soldier. A sense of delight appeared on the Captain's face. He pulled out a large serrated knife and pressed it to the soldier's chest.

"Now let us see what secrets you hold, you worthless...," the Captain trailed off as he began slowly cutting the soldier's shirt with his knife.

"You better be careful. You don't want to do something you'll regret," the soldier calmly stated. The Captain did not realize that the soldier was slowly working his hands free from his crude binding. Apparently Gerry II, the one who originally bound the soldier, did not think that they would have taken this long in securing the item. Usually the Captain was quick and ruthless.

After the Captain had sliced through the soldier's shirt he used one hand to lift up the pieces of the shirt.

"Ah huh. Here it is," he chuckled as he removed the package from the soldier's chest.

"Here see what's in here."

The Captain tossed the leather satchel

to Gerry I, who slightly fumbled the catch.
Gerry I could not believe that the Captain
would not want to take the first look.
After all, who was he to not obey a direct
order?  Gerry I found the leather tie
holding the satchel shut and untied the
two leather laces.  He opened the flap and
gently pulled the satchel apart causing a
small black void to form.  It was difficult to
see the contents of the satchel, for the
satchel was made out of a very dark color
leather.  He moved his fingers into the
black void and felt nothing.

Gerry II stepped over to him and peered
into the black void and saw black.  He
gestured for Gerry I to hand him the

satchel, which he complied.  Gerry II also reached his fingers into the small black hole.

"Well, what is in there that holds so much value?"

No response.

"Well?" the Captain stated again, getting more irritated.

"Nothing," Gerry I stated quietly.

"What? What was that you said?"

"Nothing," Gerry II stated with more volume then his fellow soldier.

"You two must be as blind as you are

stupid. Bring me the satchel," the Captain said with loud conviction.

"I guess I have to do everything myself," he stated to the soldier, who by this time had freed himself from his crudely made bonds. Gerry I walked over to the Captain with Gerry II following behind him. The Captain took the open satchel with his free hand, the other hand still holding the knife, which he used to slice open the soldier's shirt to find the satchel. Gerry I and II stood on each side of the soldier as the Captain began examining the dark leather object.

"Is this supposed to be some kind of

joke?  Am I supposed to be amused?" the Captain said aloud facing the soldier and pointing his knife at his heart and then in random places.

"If it is a joke, then the joke is on you," the soldier calmly stated to the more furious enemy Captain.

"We will see who has the last laugh when we take you back to our camp.  We will have to be a little more persuasive when we get back."

"I am running out of patience. You...take him," the Captain stated as he held his knife pointed at Gerry I.

Before Gerry I could obey, the soldier reacted with lightening quick reflexes. Grabbing the hand of the Captain, which was pointing the knife, the soldier forcefully guided the serrated knife into Gerry I's heart. After the knife blade was resting comfortably in Gerry I's heart, the soldier forced the Captain's hand to release the handle of the knife by twisting his wrist so powerfully that the Captain's wrist shattered into many pieces causing him to scream out in agony and fall many steps to his side landing on his back.

Before Gerry II could process what was happening, he received an expertly executed palm strike to the face, which shattered his maxilla and nasal column pushing fragments of bone back into his skull.

The soldier turned and slowly walked over to the Captain who was still writhing in pain.

"I told you, you did not want to do something you will regret. You should not take things that do not belong to you." With those words the soldier smashed the Captain's scrawny neck with one powerful stomp of his boot. The soldier took the dead Captain's Luger out of its holster and quickly took cover behind the tree trunk that he had just moments before been leaning up against. He listened intently and could hear two voices in the distance. The voices grew nearer.

"He sure had him screaming out already. Usually they don't make a sound until we have them back in camp." Gerry III calmly explained to Gerry IV.

"The sound he made was awful. He must be in a tremendous amount of pain." Gerry IV stated.

"Good. Then we will not have to get involved this time. I cannot stand seeing their faces as we interrogate them."

They did not notice anything different

as they continued their conversation as they entered the area where their Captain and two of their fellow soldiers lay dead.

"We heard the screams and decided to come back. We thought you were done with him Captain. Captain?" he asked after a slight pause.

Those were the last words Gerry III would say. A round from the Captain's Luger entered his left temple with a second round entering his heart. As Gerry III was falling lifelessly backward to the ground, Gerry IV was watching helplessly, his own body slowly turning in the direction of his fellow soldier. As he turned, a round from the Luger struck and lodged into his skull before his right ear, with a second round entering his upper back between the shoulder blades. He fell to the ground face first.

The soldier, confident in his safety, walked over to Gerry III and IV and emptied the remaining rounds into their skulls.

"*Move soldier!*" a voice inside his head began to yell. He dropped the Luger by the dead bodies after he had retrieved the satchel from the smashed Captain and picked up one of the loose MP40s. He scavenged for supplies, including ammo, and began exiting the gruesome scene.

*"Move soldier! ...Move your feet, soldier! Move! Move! Move!"* the voice commanded again.

The soldier quickly began making his way for the next rally point. The forest grew thicker and darker with a thick grey haze beginning to move through the trees. The soldier's eyes began to get foggy and watery.

He yawned trying to get the necessary oxygen that his body desperately needed. He could not escape the feeling of fatigue. He drifted off into the unknown.

## THE MAN

### / ./ ./ ./ ./

The man again grabbed his suit coat tightly around him during the night as he slept and the temperature became cooler. His suit pants were still wrinkled as well as his shirt, after all he was still sleeping on a park bench.

The man again stirred as the sound of more men's footsteps came closer toward him. The men's footsteps echoed loudly through the trees as they walked on the cobblestone and concrete walkway, which would lead them directly to him.

# The Cowboy

The blazing sun bore down on the already scorched earth. The red clay soil bore the cracks of the intense heat. The landscape was barren except for patches of brush. Day after day this was what the horse and rider experienced from sunrise to sunset. They had been riding for days and finally out of the hazy steaming cracked red clay soil a town appeared off in the distance.

The town was a small mining camp,

which had grown over the years. When the town began it was merely a few dozen tents with various miners and business men, but now the town has flourished and transformed into a small cosmopolitan city with many stores and shops. The city hall building had just received a small dome on top of its main building resembling the Capital building in Washington D.C. Of course there were housing structures, a few saloons, some stables, and various buildings of industry.

As the horse and rider approached the town the heat subsided and a cold wind blew down from the North West causing the brim of the rider's hat to violently shake. The wind became so violent that his horse stopped in its tracks.

"Come on boy. We are almost there." the rider calmly stated gently patting the side of his horse's neck.

"Come on. Let's go." The rider spurred on his horse.

The setting sun would be upon them. With swift strides the pair made up the distance quickly and reached the town. His coat was layered in dirt and debris from his long journey. The horse's gallop swiftly changed to a slow walk as they entered the main part of town. The rider directed the horse to the hitching post in front of the saloon. The rider dismounted and tied the horse's reins in an over hand knot around the post. He unhooked the saddlebags and swung them over his broad shoulder.

The inside of the saloon was fairly busy for this time of day. Most of the shop owners would stop by after they closed up their shops for the day. Everyone in town knew that if the store was closed the owner was more than likely to be at the saloon.

The bar was towards the left with about ten circular tables spread out throughout the establishment. Most of the tables were full with various card games in full action. The rider walked to the bar and motioned for a glass.

"What will it be stranger?" the short rotund bar keep asked with a genuine full smile.

"Anything. I've been riding for days." the rider replied.

"Okay." the bar keep replied and grabbed a bottle from under the counter pouring a small glass of it for the rider.

"That will be fifty cents."

The rider reached into the breast pocket of his filthy coat and pulled out a mint condition silver dollar and placed it on the counter.

"Keep the change." he calmly stated picking up the glass. He took a sip from the glass and turned to continue his survey of the establishment. Two tables were empty towards the back of the room. One of the tables was directly under a hanging chandelier while the other one was only illuminated by a small wall sconce with a candle. He walked over and placed his saddlebags on the dimly illuminated table. He walked to the chair at the other end of the table and sat down. He sat with his back to the wall and the dim light of the candle to his right. As he sat quietly drinking from his glass, he almost seemed to disappear into his surroundings. His filthy coat perfectly blended in with the area he chose to have a seat in. Time seemed to move slowly as the rider sat and watched the activity in the saloon rise and fall with every drink he took from the glass.

The bar keep began to get ready to close as the last few customers were winding down their game of cards.

"All right folks! I'll be closing up for the night in ten minutes! Please come settle your tabs as you exit the building!" The bar keep loudly exclaimed as to get everyone's attention with his loud jovial voice. The bar keep continued drying his drinking glasses and mugs as he waited for the customers to leave.

"Five more minutes' folks! Five more

minutes!" he exclaimed again.

The two wooden doors swung open and a group of five men entered. The group looked like they just came out of a massive dust storm. The leader wore a large woven straw like sombrero, which had a multi-colored band. He also wore a large ruby red sash across his chest. Two large .45 caliber colt peacemaker revolvers hung loosely on the man's hips. A large knife was tucked into his belt. The other men carried a knife and colt navy revolvers. One of them wore a long leather coat, one had a white puffy shirt situated under a leather vest, and the other two men wore black suits, which made them appear to be dusty filthy bankers.

The leader, the man with the sombrero, gestured to the men to find who they had come for as he walked up to the bar where the bar keep was just about to close up shop.

"I'm sorry mister, but I'm closing up for the night. You'll have to come back in the morning. We serve breakfast around 7 a.m."

"That is too bad, amigo. We have business to settle tonight."

The leader's group of men had searched the premises and located the rider at the back table. The men slowly returned to the bar. One of the men who wore a black suit leaned over to the leader and quietly told him that the rider and saddlebags were there on the far side of the room. The leader seemed pleased.

"I'm sorry sir, but you and your friends will have to come back in the morning. We are closed for the night." the bar keep stammered out completely forgetting the rider was still seated at the dimly lit table. The rider had not moved since he took his seat at the table and finished his drink. The small glass remained motionless as was the rider.

The man with the sombrero drew one of his .45 caliber colt peacemaker revolvers and emptied a round into the bar keep's chest.

"We have business that cannot wait."

The round entered the bar keep's chest with such great force, that it knocked the man backward causing him to shatter the large glass mirror behind him as he fell to the floor.

"Mis amigos, vamos. We have some business to take care of." the leader stated as he gestured the men to follow him as he began approaching the motionless rider at the back dimly lit table.

The men circled the table, standing over the seated rider and the saddlebag, which still lay out on the table. The leader pulled out one of the empty chairs and sat down, leaning backward as he propped both feet on the edge of the table. He crossed his ankles and interlocked his fingers behind his head making his arms look like two large letter Vs. He was amused, which was surprising for a man who just committed cold blooded murder.

"You thought you could escape from our little group, did you?"

A long pause.

"I told you we would find you. No matter how far you went."

The rider sat motionless.

"Oh yes, I almost forgot...you never were one for long conversations. How about another drink?"

A short pause.

"Maybe that will loosen you up; after all we have some catching up to do."

He grabbed his sombrero from his head and waved it in the air towards the bar. The man with the leather coat understood the leader's signal and walked over to the bar. He opened the side tabletop and walked behind the bar. All of the liquor bottles were neatly shelved under the bar. He grabbed a couple of bottles of whiskey and delivered them to the table where the two men sat with the others around them.

The man with the sombrero sat upright and grabbed one of the bottles. He uncorked the bottle with his teeth and spit the cork out onto the floor. While the leader was pouring the rider a glass, the man with the puffy shirt and leather vest went over to the bar and found himself a flask of burden. The rider's empty glass was now refilled and placed in front of him.

"Now we can talk...just like the old days." The leader said calmly. He took the bottle of whiskey and began drinking from the bottle.

"We were so nice to you," he began after taking a large swig from the bottle.

"We found you lying there in the brush with nothing, but those saddlebags."

He pointed over the wooden table top to

where the saddlebags still lay on the table.

"We gave you a horse and let you ride with us..."

A long dramatic pause.

"...the most notorious gang in all of the country."

"That is funny. Are you trying to make me laugh? I don't remember it that way." the rider replied as he picked up his glass and took a drink.

"The only one, or should I say ones, lying in the brush were members of your gang, who tried to take something that did not belong to them."

The eyes of the man with the sombrero stared straight at the saddlebags.

"I lost some of my best men that day. Now I am here to collect."

He reached over across the table and grabbed the saddlebags pulling it over to him. As him began to open it, the rider took another large drink from his glass, emptying the liquid from the glass into his mouth, but he did not swallow.

The leader of the gang untied the leather straps and nervously fumbled opening the leather flap. Finally the saddlebags were opened and he began to dump the contents out of the saddlebags onto the table. He began violently shaking the saddlebags again with the same result, nothing continued to come out.

"What is this? Is this some sort of trick?" the leader of the gang frantically spoke.

He dropped the saddlebags on the table and leaned across the table grabbing the rider's shirt with both hands, pulling the rider forward causing both men to be face to face.

"Where is it? Where is what was in the saddlebags you stupid son of a ...?"

Before he could finish his frantic anger filled rant, the rider struck the right side of the leader of the gang's head with his empty glass with such force that the glass shattered. Large shards of shattered glass filled the air and filled the side of the filthy man's head, embedding themselves into the filthy man's right upper cheek, right temple, and right eye socket.

Screaming in pain the leader let go of the man and stumbled backward into the man with the leather coat. After the leader loosened his grip the rider turned to his right and spit out the whiskey that he had pretended to drink moments earlier at the dimly lit candle that was next to the man that looked like a banker on his right. The whiskey created such a large intensely hot fireball that it engulfed the man's face. He instinctively reacted to the pain by putting his hands to his face, which was not a very bright idea, for now his sleeves caught on fire and in a few moments he was engulfed in flames. He tried to run outside, but was so panicked he could not tell what direction he was moving and ran into a metal lamp bracket attached to one of the support beams knocking himself unconscious as he tried to escape. The rider then grabbed the other man who looked like a banker on his left and slammed his head down onto the table top, momentarily immobilizing him as he fell to the ground.

Quickly the rider drew his revolver and unloaded two rounds in the man wearing the leather coat, who had recovered from the leader falling backwards into him. The rounds struck him in the neck and chest. The rider them fired a round into the man wearing the puffy shirt and leather vest, who was still facing away from the action and toward where the shattered mirror was behind the bar as he drank from his flask of burden. The round entered the back of his skull, killing him instantly. The man who looked like a banker who had his head rammed into the table top was beginning to stand up when a round from the rider's revolver entered his chest, lodging itself into his heart.

The rider felt a round whistle by his head as he turned to see the leader of the gang attempt to fire at him. With being blinded moments earlier the leader was unable to accurately hit his target. The rider moved slowly to the wounded man as he kept firing his weapon, soon there was only a clicking sound of an empty gun being fired. The rider pointed his revolver at the leader and from a short distance away, unloaded the last two rounds into his head.

He noticed the fire that engulfed the man who looked like a banker had began to spread throughout the back of the establishment. He quickly reloaded his revolver and then holstered it. He then quickly walked over to the table, closed the saddlebags and swung it over his shoulder. Very calmly the rider exited the building and found his horse at the hitching post in front of the burning saloon. He untied his horse and walked the horse away from the building before mounting the horse. He spurred the horse on and in moments the two of them were furiously galloping out of the town in the middle of the darkness, which was now being accented by a vibrant intense orange and yellow glow. The actions of this night were so surreal, the rider thought to himself as his horse rode on into the unknown, as if this night were a very bad and unforgettable dream.

*/ ./ ./ ./ ./ ./*

The man again grabbed his suit coat tightly around him during the night as he slept and the temperature became cooler. His suit pants were still wrinkled as well as his shirt, after all he was still sleeping on a park bench.

The man again stirred as the sound of more men's footsteps came closer toward him. The men's footsteps echoed loudly through the trees as they walked on the cobblestone and concrete walkway, which would lead them directly to him.

# The Man

The sun was brightly shining through the tree tops illuminating the city park in a brilliant glow. The many trees provided the perfect filter as the sun shone brightly down on the multitude of park visitors. Many people visited the park throughout the week with peek times usually on the weekend days or holidays. However, the city management had decided to add extra security forces that would patrol the park and keep the park patrons safe during the day and night.

The leading supervisor of the security team was taking on the role of training officer as he was patrolling the park with one of the city management new hires.

"I was told that your name was Gustaf. I have not known anyone by that name before." Albert, or as the other members of the team called him Al, said to his trainee.

"Yes it is. My parents thought that it would honor my ancestors to keep one of their names alive. To be honest, I don't know if any of them ever had that name. I don't even know where they even come from. It does not matter anyway, I would prefer it if you just called me Gus."

"All right. I did not mean to offend you. I'll call you Gus."

They walked along the marked path, which consisted of intricate designs of expertly laid cobblestones of various kinds that transitioned into a concrete walkway. There was much activity happening on every side of them as they continued on their patrol. People had begun playing games with their children, couples were having romantic picnics in the more secluded parts of the park, individuals were jogging solo and in groups, and even the animal lovers had brought their four-legged companions to the park to stretch their legs. Everything at the park seemed to fit perfectly in place.

"Now, our main goal is to keep the people safe."

"Excuse me Al, but how do we do that? There are a lot of people here."

"Gus, you are right. There are a lot of people here, but there are also a lot of us here too. We are patrolling on foot, but there are members of the force that are on bicycles and horses. They can provide back up very quickly for us in case we encounter any trouble during our patrol. Plus we have these handy-dandy walkie-talkies that allow us to be in constant contact with each other. One more thing, if life experience has taught me anything, this park is one of the safest places on the planet. I have been patrolling here for over twenty years and the only problems that I can recall this place ever having were a couple of desperate individuals who grabbed a few elderly women's purses as they sat feeding the birds and squirrels."

"Wow! That is it, I feel better know. I guess I put too much pressure on myself."

"I am sure you will do fine. There is just one more thing. A few days ago another patrol came across an individual sleeping on one of the benches. They tried to make him leave, but he started yelling in some kind of gibberish. They left him there with a warning to leave. I don't think he left. We have been assigned to stop by where he was last seen and see if he has left. I don't think he is a threat. He probably is just drunk or possibly not mentally all there. Luckily for us, the drunks and vagrants seem to move along on their own, which makes our job a whole lot easier. City management wants this park to be free of vagrants and the homeless. They have a certain image they want to convey to the community."

"Great, my first day on the job and I get to deal with an insane homeless man."

"Don't forget he could also be heavily intoxicated. Those are usually the fun ones."

Al and Gus walked on in the direction of where the man was last seen sleeping on one of the park benches. As they continued following the cobblestone and concrete walkway, they were approached by another member of the security team.

"Hey Al!" Eddie exclaimed as he came walking closer to the pair.

"Hey Eddie!" Al responded.

Al, Gus, and Eddie converged upon each other, forming a small circle.

"I was in the area and remembered that you were going to be going to see the man on your patrol, so I figured I would just follow along and lend a hand if you needed any help. Plus I did not get to meet the new hire yet. I was told that he was a very nervous short and bald man with a hump on his back. I bet he will not last the day after he sees the man."

"Eddie, this is Gus, the new hire. Gus this is Eddie, our...let us say comic relief." Al said as he pointed to Gus who was standing beside him.

"Hello." Gus politely said before continuing on.

"A short, bald nervous hunchback? That is what you thought I was? If that was supposed to be funny then you should stick to your day job."

"I am sorry, I was just kidding around. Sometimes my jokes just do not come out right.  I have been told many times that I should stick to my day job.  I heard good things about you from the other guys.  Welcome to the team and this beautiful spot of paradise." Eddie stated pointing to all of the trees that surrounded them.

"That is all right.  You are not the first one to try and give me a hard time on my first day of work.  I was just telling Al that I felt so lucky being able to deal with a homeless, possibly drunk, man on my first day on the job."

"Don't feel that bad, I had a pair of male flashers on my first day.  I tried to escort them out of the park and they decided to run.  It went from a pair of flashers to streakers in less than thirty seconds."

"That must have been a sight to see."

"Yeah, I don't think anything could prepare me for that."

"All right you two, you guys can talk as we walk. I want to get to the man before sundown and remember I will do all of the talking when we see him."

"You're the boss." Both Gus and Eddie responded in unison.

The three men entered a newer area of the park that contained fewer trees than the older sections of the park. There were many park benches laid out across the landscape, but only one contained a man sleeping. The man had grabbed his suit coat tightly around him during the night as he slept and the temperature became cooler. His suit pants were wrinkled as well as his shirt, after all he was sleeping on a park bench in the middle of the day.

The man stirred as the sound of the three men's footsteps came closer as they walked on the cobblestone and concrete walkway.

"Okay guys you stay here. I will go talk to him." Al commanded as he began to slowly approach the slumbering man.

"Excuse me sir, but you cannot sleep here. This is a private park not a hotel, which does not allow its patrons to drink alcoholic beverages openly." Al spoke to the man with a nervous calm pointing to a large brown paper bag that was stationary next to the sleeping man.

The man opened his eyes. He released his grip on his suit coat as he swung his legs outward and sat upright. After his feet were firmly on the ground, the man leaned back on the bench outstretching both arms and resting them on the back of the top of the bench. After a few minutes, the man finally spoke.

"To feel is to be, to be felt by the hand of creation can only be true to a fool who is abused."

"I do not understand sir. Maybe you

did not hear me. I said that you cannot sleep in the park." Al stated.

"Everyone laughs at the mocking clown, a lowly jester in the highest court. The tears run down upon his painted face, he falls to the Earth his comfort in his little worth."

Gus and Eddie, who were close by and could hear everything that the man was saying, looked at each other with puzzled expressions. The man paused for what seemed to be a dramatic effect in what he was saying and continued on.

"He laughs for all who reside in this dwelling..."

A loud bout of laughter came from the

man and then a more dramatic pause.

"...such a place for a fool. His duty done, the time has come to show his face to all, at the moment of revelation his destiny's to fall on his face, he turns into a disgrace."

Al was puzzled also after hearing the man's speech and did not know was to do. He gathered his wits and stepped closer to the man, who had placed his elbows on his knees and was now holding his face in is two hands.

"Sir you have to find..." Al began to say as he was interrupted by the man who again recited his poem, but with much more intense passion, which included emotional hand gestures and facial expressions as he began walking around the bench in circles.

"To feel is to be, to be felt by the hand of creation can only be true to a fool who is abused. Everyone laughs at the mocking clown, a lowly jester in the highest court. The tears run down upon his painted face, he falls to the Earth his comfort in his little worth. He laughs for all who reside in this dwelling such a place for a fool. His duty done, the time has come to show his face to all, at the moment of revelation his destiny's to fall on his face, he turns into a disgrace."

The man sat back down on the bench

giving the impression that he was physically as well as emotionally drained from his oration. Al walked back to Gus and Eddie and quietly discussed what they should do. Al had never had been in this situation before. Gus suggested that they call the police and have him arrested, while Eddie suggested that they just leave him there. After all the man was not causing any harm to anyone. Al decided to go back and talk to the man for a second time.

"All right sir. I am going to ask you to leave the park. You cannot stay here and sleep on the park benches. Is there any other place you can stay? Is there any..."

78

Once again Al was interrupted by the man who offered the following response:

"How did I get here?" The man asked in a serious tone to Al, who could not believe what he was experiencing. The man again stood and continued on animating every word.

"I can remember after my father died, being crowned king of my clan. I was their king at the age of sixteen. For years that followed I lead my people to victory in every battle we were forced to fight and peace was achieved within my clan of Toligaths and some of the surrounding clans of the country." The man paused and waved his arm as to signal the park as his kingdom.

As the man stood motionless and Al stood dumbfounded, Gus and Eddie again looked at each other in bafflement. They did not realize that two other members of the security team, the twins Phil and Bill, had ridden up behind them on their horses. Phil and Bill were part of the security team that patrol the more hard to reach areas of the park, which required the need to use horses in order to successfully patrol the area.

"Hey Eddie. We see that you and Al have come to visit the man. Isn't he a riot? I love it when he acts out every word." Phil and Bill stated in unison. It must be a twin thing, for they constantly talk at the same time and finish each other's sentences.

"Hey guys." Eddie replied. He regained his composure after being startled from hearing the twins' voices.

"Al and Gus, the newest member of our team, were assigned to get rid of the man and I tagged along to see our fearless leader in action."

"Yeah. We had the same feeling, so we decided to swing by. Oh, listen up this is a good part. The country he grew up in was unified or something" Phil said as he pointed over his horse's head to the man who was continuing on with his story.

Gus and Eddie turned their attention back to the man.

"The country that I loved and grew up in was unified for the first time since its existence. However the mood would soon change when the dreaded Tolgans invaded our land from the east. They were not stupid for they charged for the capital of my empire, the place where I lived."

"The Toll Gains, what is a Toll..." Al asked puzzled, but the man would not reply and continued on as if he was the only one standing there.

"The leader of the Tolgans was named Goligath, a strong and courageous fighter from the island off our country's eastern coast.  I remember the battle well."

The man did not show any signs of fatigue as he now became more and more intensely animated as he continued on telling his story.

"His troops attacked my men right at the break of dawn.  They were like a huge black blanket covering the countryside as they approached the castle walls.  My men were brave and fearless as they tried and succeeded in stopping the evil intruders. However Goligath would not be stopped, he pushed forward on his demon black steed.  He was slicing down my men with his wicked sword.  My best friend met the beast head on before I could get to him.

They battled each other on horseback as I approached I could see the wicked sword of Goligath lunged into Tolstan's ribs. Goligath was laughing at his evil deed as I approached him from behind. I swung my sword with the strength of my two hands. Its massive blade severed Goligath's head from his massive shoulders and it toppled to the grassy earth below. The minions of Goligath paused in their tracks as they saw his head fall to the earth followed by his body. As Goligath's minions began to run I remember yelling to my men, "Put his head on a stake and place it in front of the castle to remind everyone who is in charge. Let everyone see who is their protector and what will happen to them if they disagree and take actions upon themselves. These invasions will not be tolerated in this land or any land anymore and nevermore!" Thus Goligath's head was placed in front of the castle on a pike as a reminder to the rest of the country."

The man finished and was face to face with Al. Al had no idea on how to react and handle this situation. He became more afraid as he sensed the man was not just looking at him, but staring through him. Al began to slowly walk backward in the direction of his security team. The man did not move, but stayed motionless.

Al retreated back to Gus and Eddie, not

noticing that Phil and Bill had arrived.

"Hey boss. It looks like you just had your first experience with the man. Is it not the wildest thing you have ever experienced?" Bill stated to Al, bringing back Al's attention to the present.

"Oh hello Bill...and Phil, I didn't see you or your brother up there. How goes your patrol? Have you had any problems today?" Al stated trying to regain his composure.

"Everything is fine." The twins replied at the same time. Al did not really hear them for he was still thinking about what he had just experienced with the man. This had never happened to him before and he did not know how to handle the situation.

"For the first time in over twenty years I am at a loss for words. I do not know what to do. This guy is definitely not all there."

"Al..." Gus stated pointing back at the bench where the man was seated at earlier.

"...there is a large brown paper bag on the bench, is the man intoxicated at all?" Gus asked.

"I could not smell any alcohol on his breath or even is clothes. I think that he is as dry as the desert sand and is just fully insane. It is probably best if I go and talk with one of my supervisors to see how to proceed with this situation. We better leave this area before he does something else unpredictable that could even be dangerous."

"Look at him..." Eddie began.

"He does not seem dangerous. He is walking in circles around the bench like he is a dog trying to get comfortable to lie down and go to sleep. Plus he had lots of opportunity to hurt you if was going to. He never even laid a hand on you."

"After all he has been here for three days without any incident. What's one more day?" The twins asked to Al.

"I still think you should call the police.

From what I just witnessed that man is very unstable. He needs to be removed from this place before there is trouble and people get seriously hurt." Gus argued to the group.

"You all make valid points, but I still have to follow the chain of command. I will go talk to my supervisor when we get back from our patrol. We still have a job to do today. Now let us go and finish our patrols." Al spoke feeling more in control of the situation then he really was. After all he was the men's commanding officer and they all respected him. As the men were leaving to finish their patrols, they could hear the man begin talking to himself as he again grabbed his suit coat and curled into a sleeping position on the park bench.

"T' is the end of this story even though it has not officially begun. We see the heroes have come and gone, yet some have stayed awhile to tell their tales of courage and fear. While some have fled from fear, others have faced the creature head on. Brave men of days of old and current lives cannot be dismissed for all of them have given their life for others. This is true heroics or it could be false ethics, the reasons are yours to see. The stories might explain these antics or lead you astray, but be not confused they are only stories mostly false, but some are true."

The man looked up into the distance and saw the members of the security team walking back in the direction that they had came from. They looked like large black shadowy silhouettes that became smaller and smaller as they became further and further away, until finally they disappeared.

"Good. It was about time for that one to leave. At least this time only one of them tried to talk to me instead of all five. They seemed to stay longer than they did before. Now that they are gone I can get back to sleep. Let us see what kind of trouble I can get myself into this time."

The man said out aloud to himself as he closed his eyes and drifted off into his next adventure as the large brown paper bag fell to the ground empty.

# About The Author

Donovan Hurst graduated from San Diego State University with a Bachelor of Arts in the major field of studies of History and a minor in the field of studies of Anthropology.  He is a current member of The General Society of Mayflower Descendants and has been conducting genealogical research for over 10 years tracing back his ancestors to their ancestral homelands in Denmark, England, France, Germany, Ireland, Norway, and Scotland.